Pyro

Pyro

Monique Polak

Orca currents

ORCA BOOK PUBLISHERS

Library and Archives Canada Cataloguing in Publication

Polak, Monique
Pyro / Monique Polak.
(Orca currents)

Issued also in electronic formats.
ISBN 978-1-4598-0229-2 (bound).--ISBN 978-1-4598-0228-5 (pbk.)

I. Title. II. Series: Orca currents
PS8631.O43P97 2012   jc813'.6   C2012-902227-6

First published in the United States, 2012
Library of Congress Control Number: 2012938160

Summary: Franklin has to learn to cope with life's challenges
without setting illegal fires.

MIX
Paper from
responsible sources
FSC
www.fsc.org   FSC® C016245

*Orca Book Publishers is dedicated to preserving the environment and has
printed this book on paper certified by the Forest Stewardship Council®.*

Orca Book Publishers gratefully acknowledges the support for its
publishing programs provided by the following agencies: the Government
of Canada through the Canada Book Fund and the Canada Council for the Arts,
and the Province of British Columbia through the BC Arts Council
and the Book Publishing Tax Credit.

Cover photography by Dreamstime.com
Author photo by Monique Dykstra

ORCA BOOK PUBLISHERS
PO Box 5626, Stn. B
Victoria, BC Canada
V8R 6S4

ORCA BOOK PUBLISHERS
PO Box 468
Custer, WA USA
98240-0468

www.orcabook.com
Printed and bound in Canada.

15 14 13 12 • 4 3 2 1

For Claudia Lighter,
who's smart and sweet, and sometimes
lets me pretend she's mine

Chapter One

The broadcaster's voice crackles through the radio. "Thanks for agreeing to speak with us today, Mayor Westcott. I know you've been extremely busy dealing with the recent spate of fires in your community. For those listeners who have not been following the story, there have been eight fires this summer in Montreal West. Each one bigger and more dangerous than the last. Tell us, Mayor, what exactly are you doing to apprehend the person or persons responsible for these fires?"

My dad clears his throat. He does that when he's nervous. "First, I want to assure everyone that my team and I are doing everything we can to deal with this situation. We're working closely with the Montreal Fire Department. Our community has one of the best volunteer fire brigades in the country. But I also want to tell you"—Dad stops here to take a breath—"that this situation is serious. Whoever's been lighting these fires is a heartless monster. I repeat—a heartless monster. A person without any feeling whatsoever for the well-being of others. And we will stop him—or her—or them.

"I'd like to take this opportunity to urge your listeners to contact us immediately if they notice anything suspicious—anything at all. I also want to urge your listeners to inspect the periphery around their homes to ensure they have not left out any flammable substances, things like paint thinner or gasoline. It's especially important to check sheds and garages. Any area that's accessible to an intruder. So far, thank god, no lives have been lost. We want to keep it that way."

"Thank you, Mr. Mayor. Our thoughts are with you and the people of Montreal West. We wish you luck as you continue your investigation. Why don't we give listeners the phone number to call if they have anything suspicious to report?"

I turn off the radio as my dad rattles off the number at city hall.

I adjust the pillow under my head and think how, if I didn't know my dad, I'd think Mayor Westcott was pretty together. Only I know better.

How can my dad catch a criminal when he doesn't even know what's going on under his own roof?

I hear the front door open. The fumes wafting upstairs tell me it's Mom. She never used to wear perfume or get her hair done so often. "Franklin?" she calls out. "You home, honey?"

I hate how she calls me "honey." That's what she calls *him* too. The guy she's been getting it on with. I've read the emails. It didn't take a genius to figure out her password: cupcake. Mom collects stuff with cupcakes on it—cupcake plates, cupcake potholders. If it's got a cupcake on it, Mom owns it.

I've followed her a couple of times at night too. She says she wants exercise, but I know better. She's been going for walks so she can phone him.

"Hey, honey," I'd heard her say, her voice all sweet and drippy. It was like honey, now that I think about it. "I just wanted to tell you how fun that was yesterday."

If Dad were any kind of investigator, he'd be looking at her emails or checking the cell-phone bill.

The thing with Dad is, he can't see the signs. The emails. Mom's sudden interest in after-dinner walks. Two weeks ago was their wedding anniversary. Dad gave her a mushy card from the drugstore. She didn't give him anything. And Dad didn't say a word about it.

She's coming upstairs now. When she knocks at my door, I don't bother answering. I want her to think I'm asleep.

"Franklin? You in there?" she says.

If I don't say something now, she's gonna barge right in.

"Yeah. I'm resting," I say.

"Mind if I come in, honey?"

She doesn't wait for me to answer. She just lets herself in and plunks herself down on the end of my bed. I roll over. I don't want to have to look at her. "How many gardens did you weed today, Franklin?"

"Eleven. I think."

"Good for you. That's quite a business you've got going. I'm proud of you, honey."

"Don't call me honey."

"Why ever not, hon—?" She stops herself. "I'm thinking of making meat sauce with sausage." She knows it's my favorite. She's waiting for me to say something, but I don't.

"Your cousin Jeff is in town."

"He is?" I haven't seen Jeff since Christmas.

"I invited him for supper. He'll be here in half an hour. Want to rest till then?" She leans across the bed. Even though

I'm facing away from her, I can feel her stretching out her arms. "How 'bout a little massage, honey?"

Honey? "Don't touch me!" I growl.

"Fine," Mom says. "You go ahead and rest up. I'm going to get that sauce started."

"Mom?"

"Yes, Franklin?" Her voice sounds suddenly hopeful.

"I wish you wouldn't wear so much of that perfume. It really stinks up the place."

Chapter Two

Mom and Dad sit at opposite ends of the dining-room table. Jeff and I are in between, facing each other. When I was a kid, there was nothing I liked more than hanging out with my big cousin. Jeff is like the big brother I never had. Thinking back on it, he probably thought I was a pain in the butt, following him and his pals around. But if he minded, Jeff never said so.

I took it hard when Jeff moved to Toronto for university. He was back in Montreal last summer, but this summer he's working in Toronto. He's only home for the weekend.

"No one makes a better spaghetti sauce than you, Aunt Moira," Jeff tells Mom when he asks for a second helping.

Mom beams.

"Anyone hear me on the radio today?" Dad wants to know. "How'd I sound?"

"I didn't know you were going to be on the radio, Ted," Mom tells him.

"I mentioned it this morning." Dad doesn't seem to get that it's a bad sign that his own wife didn't bother listening to the interview.

"I heard you," I say to my spaghetti. "You sounded kinda nervous."

"I am nervous. We need to catch whoever is starting these fires." Dad pounds his fist on the table. "Otherwise, I might not get re-elected."

"Of course you'll be re-elected, Ted. Everyone thinks you're a wonderful mayor." Mom smiles at Dad across the table. Her smile seems forced.

Dad wipes his face with his hands as he gets up from the table. "Speaking of getting re-elected, I'd better get a move on. I don't want to be late for the town council meeting. Sorry not to have more time to catch up, Jeff."

"Well, then I guess I'll go for my walk," Mom says.

Honey must be burning up waiting for her phone call.

About five seconds after Dad leaves, Mom is out the door too. I see her from the dining-room window. She's already on her cell.

I'm glad I've got Jeff to distract me. And apple pie with vanilla ice cream. Jeff serves himself a double scoop. Maybe he doesn't get enough to eat in Toronto.

Jeff rests his elbows on the table. "So what's up, little cuz?" Jeff has always called me that. At just under five feet, I am little for a fourteen-year-old. I'm sensitive about my height, but I've never minded Jeff calling me "little cuz."

"Same old same old. How's it going in TO?"

"It's good. Lots of opportunities in my field." Jeff works in film production. He wants to be a producer. From what he's told me, his job is mostly picking up takeout food and coffee for people on the set. "Listen, Franklin, I want to ask you something." Jeff sounds serious. I hope his question doesn't have anything to do with Mom and Dad. Mom and her brother—Jeff's dad—are pretty tight.

Maybe my Uncle Ron knows about Honey. Maybe Uncle Ron said something to Jeff.

I take a deep breath. "Fire away."

Jeff looks at me funny when I say that. "Fire away," he says, repeating my words. "You still doin' crap like that, Franklin?"

I know exactly what Jeff means. He wants to know if I'm still playing with fire. The way we did when we were kids.

"Who, me?" I say, shrugging my shoulders.

"Does that mean no?" Jeff asks.

"Yeah…I mean no."

Jeff takes a big spoon of ice cream. "Tell me, little cuz, that you're not lighting those fires in Montreal West."

"I'm not lighting those fires in Montreal West."

Jeff relaxes into his chair.

I've told him what he wants to hear.

Later, when we're loading the dish-washer, the subject comes up again.

"Remember that time we lit the bag of corn chips?" Jeff laughs out loud at the memory.

"That was crazy. Who knew corn chips were a fire starter?"

"Correction," says Jeff. "Who knew the four-portion-size bag of corn chips were a fire starter? Nothing happened when we lit the single portion bag."

"Man, that was something!" I say. "Almost as good as when you turned your mom's can of hairspray into a blowtor—" The memory makes me laugh so hard, I can't finish my sentence.

Jeff nudges my arm. "My mom was pretty ticked off when she couldn't find her hairspray. We had some good times, didn't we, little cuz?"

"We sure did. Though you weren't exactly a good influence."

That makes us both start laughing all over again.

"So what else you doing this weekend?" I ask Jeff.

"I'm seeing some of the guys I used to hang with. I'm having breakfast tomorrow with Terry. You remember him?"

"Big guy? Kind of full of himself? Used to call me squirt?"

"That's him. Did you know he joined the volunteer fire brigade? He's aiming to get a job with the Montreal Fire Department. It's all he talks about. The guy's obsessed."

"Pretty cool!" I say. I don't tell Jeff what I'm thinking—how his old pal Terry and I have something in common.

Chapter Three

Jeff sticks around to check out my new skateboard. "Everything okay around here, little cuz?" he asks when I walk him to the door.

"Sure."

"Your folks seemed a little…well, strange with each other."

"Nah, everything's fine."

"Listen," Jeff says, punching my arm. "If you ever need to talk, you can always call."

"Thanks for the offer."

I'm sprawled out on the couch, chilling. If it wasn't July and hot and dry out, I'd build a fire in our old brick fireplace.

I shouldn't have told Jeff he was a bad influence. He wasn't the one who got me hooked on fire. I was hooked way before the corn-chip and spray-can tricks.

Dad got me hooked. Mr. Mayor himself.

My first memory of fire has to do with this fireplace. I used to love watching Dad start a fire. Dad is the kind of person who's always on the go. Even when I was little, he'd head off to one meeting or another. Or he'd be on the phone doing city business. But when Dad made a fire, he was one-hundred-percent present. It was the only time he wasn't distracted.

I'd sit right here on the couch (in those days the couch was maroon—now it's got this kooky cupcake fabric Mom picked out). Dad would be on his knees in front of the fireplace. He'd tell me exactly what he was doing. "First you gotta scrunch up newspaper—like this. You payin' attention, son?" Dad would show me the balls of newspaper. "If they come undone," he'd say, "they're no good."

"Can I try?" I used to ask him.

"Fire's a powerful thing, Franklin. It creates, but it destroys too. You're not big enough yet to light fires," Dad would tell me. "But how 'bout you scrunch up some of that newspaper? Nice and tight, okay?"

I'd try so hard to get the balls of newspaper right.

"This one's a little loose, Franklin. Really scrunch it up."

Mom would be on the couch, reading a romance novel. Every once in a while, she'd look up from her book and smile. I think she liked to see us bonding. Dad wasn't the mayor yet. He was just a city councilor, but already he was away a lot.

"Next you need to make a teepee with the kindling." Dad would pile kindling into a small teepee. After that, he'd add some small logs, laying them against the teepee, but not so hard that the teepee would fall over.

And then…my favorite part. Dad would light a long match, toss it in and slam the glass door of the fireplace shut. I'd press my face against the glass and watch as all that newspaper would burst into a giant blue-and-orange flame. I'd never seen anything more beautiful.

It wasn't just the appearance of the fire I loved. It was also the sound. I loved the crackling as the fire spread, especially if the wood was damp. And the smell, the delicious aroma of wood smoke.

"It's getting smoky in here," Mom would complain from the couch. "The smoke detector's going to go off. And I'm not putting down my book to deal with it."

"You and your romances," Dad would tease her. "You'd let this house go up in flames if you were reading one of those books. Aren't I romantic enough for you?"

I remember other fires too. There were the bonfires Dad and Uncle Ron made when our families rented a cottage together in the Laurentians. Sometimes, usually after they'd put away a couple of beers, Dad and Uncle Ron would let us use bulrushes to light the bonfire. Man, that was fun! Nothing beats a flaming bulrush!

Mom and Aunt Lena would pack potatoes and corn in tinfoil, and we'd roast them over the fire pit. Jeff and I would spend the whole day hunting for just the right twigs for roasting marsh-mallows. They had to be long but not so thin our marshmallows might fall off and disappear into the flames. To this day, nothing tastes better to me than roasted potatoes and corn, or a marshmallow charred black on the outside, hot and gooey inside.

Mom says when I was little, I spent hours watching the fire in our fireplace or in those fire pits. She says it used to relax me.

The funny thing is, it still does.

I'm surprised when Dad's truck pulls into the driveway. What's he doing back so soon?

"Hey, Franklin," he says when he sees me on the couch. "The meeting broke up early. Where's your mom?"

"Still out walking, I guess."

Dad sighs. "She's been taking an awful lot of walks lately, hasn't she?"

For the first time, I wonder if maybe—just maybe—Dad isn't as out of it as he seems.

Chapter Four

I was right about Dad.

I'm upstairs when Mom gets in. It is nearly 9:30 by then. The argument starts almost instantly. Then it builds in intensity the way some fires do.

"What the heck's been going on, Moira?"

"I don't know what you're talking about. I thought you had a council meeting."

"Don't go changing the subject. Moira, you've gotta level with me. There's someone else, isn't there?"

I try putting my pillow over my head, but they're too loud. Besides, part of me wants to hear what she's going to say.

"That's not what this is about."

"What's this about, then?" I can't tell from Dad's voice if he's angry or sad.

"We've grown apart," Mom tells him. "That's what this is about." She's using the voice she used with me when I was little and I skinned my knee. The I-can-make-it-all-better voice. Only she can't make this better.

"No, that's not wh…what this is about," Dad sputters. "This is about you, Moira. It's about you cheating on *us*."

When Dad says *us*, I know he means me too. I wonder if Dad's right. Has Mom been cheating on me? Is that how it works when you have a kid?

Mom doesn't say anything. She doesn't say she hasn't been cheating, or that this is a terrible misunderstanding. That she'd never cheat on *us*.

I wish she'd say something, because her silence is only getting Dad more worked up. "You know what you are, Moira? You know what you are? You're rotten to the core!"

I sit up in my bed when he says that. It's occurred to me lately that my mom might not have the best character, but *rotten to the core* is going too far.

You'd think Mom would object, but she doesn't. Maybe she thinks it's true.

One of them is crying now. It could be Dad, but I can't tell for sure. I've never heard him cry before—not even when Grandpa died two years ago.

"I'll leave," Mom says. "If that's what you want."

I hear gulping. It is Dad who's been crying. Now his voice is hard as steel. "You will not leave, Moira. Not until after the election. What would people think if the mayor's wife—?"

Now Mom does something I wouldn't expect from her. She laughs. "What would people think?" she says in a decent imitation of Dad. "Don't you see that's what's wrong around here? If you cared more about the people you live with—about me and Franklin— I might not have fallen in love with someone else."

My chest hurts when she says that.

"And, by the way, I'm not just the mayor's wife. I'm my own person. Which is something else you've lost sight of, Mr. Mayor."

Now Dad is howling like some half-dead animal. I want to tell him to stop.

I want to tell him she's not worth it. But I can't bear the idea of seeing the two of them right now. And I definitely can't listen to any more of this crap.

I need to get out of here. I need to forget everything I just heard. I grab my black hoodie and head for the back stairs. Dad's howling is louder when I reach the ground floor. Mom is telling him something in that make-it-all-better voice, but I won't listen anymore.

In my head, I'm thinking *la la la, la la la*. Really loud. Get me out of here. Now.

I push open the back door and take a deep gulp of summer air. That helps. It's as if I couldn't breathe inside. I've never heard Mom and Dad fight like that. Usually they let things smolder. Maybe this is what happens if the smoldering goes on too long.

The crickets are singing. I could go over to Jeff's, but then I'd have to tell him what's going on.

No, I'll keep walking till my head clears. I'll try to relax.

Who am I kidding? There's only one thing that'll help me relax—and it isn't a walk.

There are hardly any lights on inside the houses I pass. Montreal West isn't exactly full of night owls. So many of the people who live here are old. I'm getting close to Elizabeth Ballantyne, my old elementary school. I spot a metal trash can at the edge of the schoolyard. Perfect.

The wind picks up, carrying with it some brochures someone dropped. I reach out and catch them. It's as if the wind wants in on my plan. Wind and fire make a powerful pair.

I reach into the front pocket of my jeans for matches.

Though the only light is the pale yellow from the streetlamp, I can see there's stuff inside the trash can.

Cigarette packets, more brochures, plastic water bottles. I scrunch up the brochures the wind brought me. Just like Dad showed me.

Then I light a match—oh, that feels good—and toss it into the trash can. I take two steps back without lifting my eyes from the trash can.

There's a *whoosh* as the fire starts, then crackling as it spreads inside the trash can.

A light goes on in the back room of one of the houses that borders the school property. It's time for me to get out of here.

I shuffle sideways, keeping my back to the wire fence that surrounds the school-yard. I keep away from the streetlamps.

I don't go far. Fire starters never do. We don't want to miss the show.

Smoke billows from the top of the trash can now, but no flames.

I hear the sharp whine of the fire engine's siren in the distance. Whoever spotted me must have phoned 9-1-1.

The volunteer fire brigade will be wasting its time. This fire is going to put itself out.

Not all of them do.

Chapter Five

When I get home, the lights are out. Dad's truck and Mom's car are both in the driveway. Could they have sorted things out?

But I know nothing's been sorted out when I take the back stairs and hear Mom whispering in the living room. She's on her cell phone, probably filling Honey in on the latest developments.

Upstairs, Dad is in their bedroom, also on the phone. I can hear him bellowing from the hallway. He must be talking to the volunteer fire chief. I hear him say, "You're sure, then, that everything's okay out there? No damage? What about clues? Did you scour the area for clues? Hmm, that's interesting. All right, then, let me know if you need me. Call at any hour."

For a man whose wife has been getting it on with some other guy, Dad sounds pretty good.

Somehow, I managed to fall asleep and stay asleep till morning. When I first wake up, I don't remember how screwed up my life is. The sun is coming through my blinds, making stripes on the bedspread. It's Sunday. I have no gardens to weed.

Then I hear shuffling noises coming from the hallway where the big closet is.

There's a loud *clunk*, and Mom says, "Oops." Now I hear her dragging what has to be her suitcase out of the closet.

I consider staying in bed and never getting up again. But I have to pee. Badly.

I walk right past her. I keep my head down so I don't have to make eye contact.

"Franklin, honey," she says, but I keep walking. "We need to talk."

"I need to pee," I mutter.

"Then afterward."

When I leave the bathroom, she's standing in the middle of the hallway, blocking my way. She's got one hand on her suitcase. "I'm leaving, Franklin," she says, as if it's not a big deal. "It's just temporary. Till your dad and I can work things out."

I know that isn't true. Not with Honey in the picture.

"Okay," I tell her.

Mom's eyes are red-rimmed, like a rabbit's. Maybe she's been crying all night. If she has, I don't feel sorry for her. She's the one who's leaving.

Dad is in the kitchen, toasting himself a slice of whole-wheat bread the way he does every morning. "Morning, son," he says, as if nothing's wrong. As if his wife isn't upstairs packing her suitcase.

"Morning, Dad. Was there another fire last night? I thought I heard the fire engine out there…when I was, er, dozing off."

Dad catches his toast in midair as it pops out of the toaster. "Yeah," he says, without looking at me, "there was another fire. This was small bones though. Trash can fire in the schoolyard at Elizabeth Ballantyne. Good news is a lady who lives nearby got pictures of the punk who did it." Dad rubs his hands together. "First big lead in the case."

"Oh," I say, trying to keep my voice level. "That's good."

I can hear Mom upstairs opening and closing her dresser drawers. Dad doesn't say anything about Mom leaving. "If we can catch this wack-job before the election, it'd be good news for me." Dad rubs his hands together again.

Mom must be done packing, because now I hear her suitcase thumping down the stairs.

A minute later, she is standing at the kitchen door. Her eyes look even redder than before. "I'm sorry," she says, looking first at me, then at Dad. "Really I am. I just don't see another way. Franklin, I'll phone you later. We'll get together for supper sometime this week, okay?"

I shrug my shoulders.

"Well, then, I guess I'll be go…ing." I don't care that her voice cracks.

Dad is standing by the kitchen counter, shifting his weight from one foot to the other, but otherwise not moving.

He should do something. He should tell her she can't go, that she has a responsibility to us. But all he does is stare at his toast like some zombie.

Mom must be halfway down the block when he finally speaks. And what he says has nothing to do with her. "I don't want you to miss Sunday school again today, Franklin."

"Sunday school?" I shouldn't be shouting, but I can't believe this. Mom is moving out, and that's all Dad has to say? And why is he talking to me like I'm ten years old? I haven't gone to Sunday school in three years!

"Things have got to change around here, Franklin." Dad sounds old and tired. I really don't want to go to Sunday school. But there's something I want to do even less—and that's stay home with Mr. Mayor.

"All right. I'll go."

I expect Dad to tell me to change out of my baggy T-shirt, but he doesn't. He also says nothing when I leave the house with my skateboard. Maybe he's just relieved I haven't put up more of a fight about Sunday school. Or maybe he's too miserable to notice.

Mrs. Ledoux, who's married to Father Ledoux, runs Sunday school. Even in summer, she has these rosy cheeks that make her look like she just got in from tobogganing. "Franklin," she says, when she spots me. "What a pleasure to see you this morning, dear. Perhaps I can fill you in on what you've missed the last few Sundays."

I don't point out the obvious—that three years' worth of Sundays add up to more than a few.

"We're preparing for a talent show. It's a fundraiser for our sister church in Kenya. Have you got a talent, Franklin, that you'd like to share with others?"

Mrs. Ledoux's question actually makes me laugh out loud. What I'm thinking is my only talents are skateboarding—and lighting fires.

I nearly jump when Mrs. Ledoux asks, "How would you like to work on the *lighting*, Franklin?"

Chapter Six

Working on the lighting isn't exactly work. There are only two sets of lights to operate—the ceiling lights and one wobbly old spotlight.

I've got the spotlight on this girl, Tracy. I haven't seen her around, so she must have just moved here, or she goes to one of those snooty girls' schools downtown.

Tracy plays the ukulele. It's a dorky-looking instrument (it looks like a Fisher-Price guitar). It doesn't help that the ukulele is hot pink. Though I have to admit it makes okay music. Tracy doesn't have a bad voice either. She's singing that old Beatles song "Let It Be."

At least she *was* singing it. Because she suddenly stops—smack in the middle of a line.

Mrs. Ledoux rushes over. "Is something wrong, dear?"

"Uh...uh," she says.

Mrs. Ledoux pets Tracy's head as if she's a small dog. Then Mrs. Ledoux claps her hands. "We're going to take a short break. Why don't the rest of you get some fresh air?"

I'm not in the mood for fresh air. Besides, I was just getting comfortable on my stool behind stage.

"Was it stage fright?" I hear Mrs. Ledoux ask Tracy.

Tracy doesn't answer; she just sniffles. Now I'm regretting not getting that fresh air.

"I like the sound of your ukulele," Mrs. Ledoux is saying. "And you have a wonderful voice, dear. But if it's too much for you to be on stage, we can find another way for you to contribute to the talent show."

"I…I'd rather not give up," Tracy says, but then she starts sniffling again. "I just get really nervous when everyone's looking at me."

"It sounds like stage fright," Mrs. Ledoux tells her. "You know, the only way to deal with it is to get right back on stage and try again. But you might prefer to wait till next Sunday. Give yourself some time."

Tracy sucks in her breath. "No, I'd like to try again today."

Later, when Tracy starts strumming that pink ukulele and singing

"Let It Be" again, I direct the spotlight so it's not right on her face. Even so, Tracy freezes all over again. This time, some kids snicker. And then Tracy goes running out of the church basement.

"I need a volunteer to go after her," Mrs. Ledoux says. "I'd go myself, but I can't leave the rest of you."

No one volunteers.

"Franklin!" I can't believe Mrs. Ledoux is calling my name. This must be her way of punishing me for missing three years of Sunday school.

I think about saying I won't go. But Mrs. Ledoux is not the sort of person who takes no for an answer. So I get up from my stool.

I've never been good with feelings. Maybe it's in my genes. I mean, look at my dad.

Anyway, when I spot Tracy by the bike rack behind the church, I don't know what to do or say. She's unlocking her bike, and for a minute I think about waiting till she's gone. I can tell Mrs. Ledoux I looked everywhere, but there was no sign of Tracy.

But Tracy spots me. "If you're here to tell me to come back in, I'm not going!" She's got her hands on her hips, and you'd think from her tone that it's my fault she got stage fright.

"I didn't come here to tell you anything," I say.

"So why are you here, then?"

Because I don't know what else to say, I tell her, "That ukulele is the dorkiest instrument I ever saw."

Tracy has wavy hair the color of fire. When she laughs, she looks, well, pretty.

"But you have an okay voice," I say. "And that dorky thing makes decent music."

Tracy straps her ukulele case (it's pink too) onto the back of her bike, but she doesn't get on. She looks at me, which makes *me* feel like running away. "I never saw you here before. What are you?" she finally says. "A Sunday school dropout?"

"I guess. My dad made me go today. My mom moved out this morning." I don't know why I'm telling her this. I wish I could take back the part about my mom, but it's too late.

"That sucks," Tracy says. "It makes stage fright seem not so bad. Look, I gotta go. I'll see you next Sunday, okay?" She pats her ukulele case. "Good luck with the mom thing."

The last thing I feel like doing is going back to the church basement and reporting to Mrs. Ledoux, so I take off on my skateboard. I half expect to see Tracy, but I don't. Moving helps take my mind off my mom and what I told Tracy.

There's hardly any traffic on Sunday morning, so it doesn't take me long to reach the northwest edge of town.

It borders on an old golf course. People have been fighting over this strip of land since before I was born. Some old-timers want to bring back the golf course. A group of businesspeople wants to build condos, and some environmentalists want to turn the area into a park. The three groups are so busy bickering that the land has been sitting stagnant for ages.

No one pays attention to the giant sign that says *No Trespassing*. In winter, cross-country skiers and snowshoers come here for exercise. This time of year, the land is covered with tall yellow and green grasses that scratch your legs. Sometimes there are other kids out here, but today the whole place is mine.

I stretch my arms and take a deep breath of the air, which feels softer than the air in town. It's nice and dry out, perfect weather for what I'm about to do.

I've read online about how farmers set grass fires on purpose. They burn fields that are depleted. It's a way to enrich the soil. The farmers destroy a field to help bring it back to life. Maybe someday I should get my own farm.

I've got a nice fat wad of lint in my back pocket. I'm the one in our family who takes the clothes from the dryer and folds them. Mom always reminds me to empty the lint catcher. "Some of the worst house fires start because people let the lint collect," she'll say. I guess now she won't be around to remind me.

Once Mom mentioned lint fires, I started collecting the stuff. And she was right. Lint is an amazing fire starter. It's better than twigs because it's more compact and easier to stash.

I take the lint from my pocket and fluff it with my fingers, since it's gotten squished. It smells like home, like our laundry room in the basement. Suddenly, I get a wave of…of…I don't know what.

Some bad uncomfortable feeling. I need to make that feeling go away.

I know what I'm about to do will help, because the feeling I get when I start a fire makes everything else go away.

There's not a cloud in the sky. My breath quickens as I fish the matches out of my other pocket. I strike the match. Even that first small spark—the sight of it, the familiar sulphur smell—gives me a rush.

When I light the wad of lint, it catches instantly. I toss it as far as I can into the tall grass. I watch as it sails through the air like a flaming bird and then disappears into the grass.

At first, I don't see anything. But I smell the sweet scent of burning grass. Then, a minute or two later, I see the first small plume of pale gray smoke. I watch as it thickens and gets blacker.

I'm like a farmer enriching the soil. No one ever gets hurt from the fires

I've set, unless you count me burning my fingertips. But that was back when I didn't know anything.

The fire spreads quickly. There's smoke and flames that are at least a foot taller than the grass. Orange-yellow flames stand out against the blue sky. The smoke makes soft gray clouds. If I were a painter, I'd paint this scene.

Sometimes I wonder about that other guy. The other fire starter.

Does he ever feel like a painter too?

Chapter Seven

I get another rush when I hear the fire engine's siren and a bigger rush when the gleaming red-and-silver truck screeches up to the old golf course. Look at what I've done! Me, Franklin Westcott! So what if I'm not big or built like a fire truck? Little guys can make big things happen too. We've just got to use our brains—and our imaginations.

To anyone who sees me now, I could be any kid out on my skateboard on a Sunday afternoon. In fact, a dozen or so other kids have come over on their skateboards or bikes, drawn by the fire engine's siren or the sharp smell of smoke. There's an old couple too. They were probably out taking a walk when they heard the fire engine. And there's Bob, this toothless guy who spends his days walking up and down the streets of Montreal West. He looks through people's trash for empty bottles to cash in at the grocery store. No one can resist a fire.

Most of the guys on the volunteer brigade are my dad's age or older, but there are some younger ones too. One is standing at the back of the truck, rubbing his eyes. Maybe he was sleeping in when his beeper went off. I know from Dad that that's how it works—every volunteer has to carry a beeper with him at all times.

There's Jeff's friend, Terry. He is a big guy with a shaved head and tattoos up his neck. He's first off the truck. When he lands on the ground, I see him look around. I know he wants people to notice him. He must think he's Russell Crowe in that old movie *Gladiator*. He doesn't bother looking at me. To a guy like Terry, I'm invisible. Terry uses his hand for a visor and looks out at the grass. "This one's spreading quick!" he calls to the others. "But we've seen worse! 'Member that grass fire last year?"

Mr. Duffy, an older man who owns the hardware store on Westminster Avenue, is the chief of the volunteer fire brigade. I'm used to seeing him in a white apron—usually with a screw dangling between his lips. It's always strange to see him in his fire-resistant suit, big black helmet and rubber boots.

"All right, boys," he tells the others, his voice tense. "Let's go get her. Folks," he calls out to those of us who have gathered near the fire truck, "out of our way, please. You need to let us do our work here."

People step back, but they don't lift their eyes from the fire.

The others have jumped off the truck too. When the driver engages the pump, it makes a whirring sound. The volunteers pull out the giant gray hose line that's stored on the side of the truck. Terry is at the front, his face red and dripping with sweat.

"Do you suppose it was that maniac again?" I hear the old lady ask her husband.

"Could be," he says. "On the other hand, it could've been an accident. Someone might've simply dropped a cigarette butt out there."

"I don't think a cigarette butt could make a fire like this," I can't resist saying.

The man looks me up and down. Is he wondering whether I could be the maniac? But then he gives me a friendly smile. "You're probably right, young man."

"We should get home," his wife says. "The smoke is hurting my eyes."

"Just a little longer," the man tells her.

She nudges him. "You might be seventy, Stanley, but inside, you're still a kid."

Terry is barking orders at the other volunteers. You'd think he was in charge, not Mr. Duffy. "Over here, now! I said now!"

My dad's truck pulls up behind the fire engine. He rushes out of his truck and toward the fire. One of the volunteers holds out his hand to block Dad's way. "You need to stay away and let us do our job."

"I'm the mayor."

"It doesn't matter who you are. Back off—for your own safety!"

Dad stomps over to where the rest of us are standing.

"Hey, Franklin," Dad says when he notices me in the small crowd. "Weren't you supposed to be at Sunday school?"

"I was there. I'm working on the talent show. It's a fundraiser for a sister church in…"

Dad is hardly listening. Like everyone else's, his eyes are glued to the fire. Most of the flames are already swallowed up by the water, but there's still smoke hanging in the air.

"Looks like the squad's got this under control," Dad says. "It's a good thing this didn't happen near the old clubhouse. The only damage seems to be to the grass. Mind you, it's a big patch."

People head home. The old lady is holding her handkerchief like a gas mask over her mouth and nose. Her husband is holding on to her elbow, but before they go, he peers over his shoulder for one last look at the fire. He waves when he catches me looking at him.

When the fire is out and the volunteers are trudging back to the truck, Dad claps each of them on the shoulder. "Nice work," he says.

The spectators who are left give the volunteers a round of applause. "Thank you," someone in the crowd calls out.

Terry takes a bow. What a jerk!

Dad offers me a ride, but I tell him I'd rather skateboard.

I've got one foot on my skateboard when someone taps my shoulder. I thought Terry didn't know who I was.

"Hey, kid," he says. It's the first time he hasn't called me *squirt*. "I want to offer my condolences about your old lady moving out." But the look on Terry's face isn't too sympathetic.

"Thanks," I tell him, "but I've got to go."

Terry shakes his head. "It must be a real bummer for you. I wondered why she was hanging out so much over by the beauty salon."

"I don't know what you're talking about."

As I take off on my skateboard, I remember how Dad said "Nice work" to the volunteer firefighters. Of course, he meant Terry too.

I'm the one who deserved the compliment. They put out the fire, but hey, I'm the one who started it.

Chapter Eight

It's Wednesday, and I'm meeting Mom for supper at the Acropolis. I can't say I'm in the mood to hang out with her, but I am in the mood for souvlaki on pita.

Dad is watching the news when I leave. "Have yourself a good night, Franklin," he calls from the cupcake sofa. He hasn't mentioned Mom since she left on Sunday. When I told him I was meeting her for supper, he just nodded like a robot. Sometimes I don't blame Mom for falling for somebody else.

Everything about the Acropolis is blue and white, even the porch outside. Bob is standing there, sucking on a cigarette. He's got spiky hair and a sunburned face that's wrinkled from being outside all day. I don't bother saying hi. He's busy talking to himself. "That's what I told her," I hear him say, "but she wouldn't listen. She never listened." What a loser!

I smell Mom's perfume before I see her. She's sitting by the window, drinking a glass of white wine. Her hair is perfectly straight. She stands up when she sees me come in. "Hey, Franklin," she says, moving in for a hug.

I duck to dodge the hug and sit down across from her. "Hey, Mom."

"How're you doing, Franklin? How's your dad?" It bugs me that she sounds like she cares, even though I know she doesn't.

I don't like the feeling of her eyes on my face. "We're great. Just great."

Mom doesn't get sarcasm. She gives me this sad smile. How, I wonder, am I going to get through this meal?

Luckily, the waitress comes to take our order. Souvlaki pitas and a Greek salad for two, thank you very much, and yes, we're done with the menus. "Is it just the two of you tonight?" the waitress asks. "Mom and son date night?"

I nearly choke on my water.

"That's right," Mom says in a too-bright voice. "Date night."

Mom unfolds her blue and white napkin. There's a stubby white candle in a blue candleholder on our table. The wick is low, but I study the flame, which is blue and steady.

"I heard you went to Sunday school."

"Who told you that?"

"Joan mentioned it." Joan is Mrs. Ledoux. "She said you went out of your way to help a girl who had stage fright."

"I didn't go out of my way. Mrs. Ledoux made me do it."

Mom smoothes the napkin on her lap. "I guess she left out that part." She reaches a hand across the table. I pull my hands back and stuff them in my pockets. The last thing I want to do is hold hands with my mother.

"You know, Franklin," Mom says, lowering her voice, "I worry about you. About the kind of person you're becoming."

"Isn't it a little late for that?"

Mom bites her lip. "Look, Franklin. You and I need to, well, start over. Find our way back to each other."

"Are you talking about you and me, or you and Dad?" I don't realize I've raised my voice until two women sitting at a nearby table turn to look.

I glare at them, and they go back to their own conversation.

"No," Mom says, "I'm talking about us, Franklin. You and me. It's my fault entirely. I've been, well, I guess you could say, distracted."

That makes me laugh. "Distracted? That's the understatement of the year."

That's when Mom starts tearing up. I refuse to feel sorry for her. If she wants to cry right here in the Acropolis, let her. What do I care?

Mom dabs her eyes with her napkin. I don't need to look at the two ladies next to us to know they are lapping this up like it's some reality show. *Your Mother's a Dummy. And Your Dad's No Better. No Wonder You Start Fires.*

Just when I think things can't get any worse, I notice this guy walking into the Acropolis. His hair (shoulder-length, blond) reminds me of the guys on the covers of Mom's romance books.

Only this guy's wearing a shirt. The heroes on the covers of Mom's books are always bare-chested and built like Schwarzenegger. Why is this guy coming over to our table? And why is Mom blushing like a girl in grade two?

I relax when I realize I know the guy. It's James. Mom's hairdresser. He's been doing her hair since forever. When I was a kid, she'd make me go to the salon with her. Man, was that boring.

"James? What are you doing here?" Mom's smile doesn't look small or sad or forced. I guess over the years, she and James have gotten friendly. Does that mean he knows about her and Dad?

James reeks of hairspray. When he smiles, you can see all his teeth. "Well, you mentioned you'd be having dinner here with Franklin tonight and so…" James lets his voice trail off. "You two mind if I pull up a chair?"

"I don't mind," Mom says. "Is it okay with you, Franklin? I know we were having mother-son time."

"I don't mind." Actually, I'm relieved. Now Mom will have someone else to talk to.

The waitress comes with the Greek salad and our souvlakis. I take a giant bite out of mine. I can feel the tzatziki dripping down my chin.

James brings a chair over to Mom's side of the table. "You smell nice," he tells her. Then he looks up at me. "You're looking good, Franklin. Is that your skateboard out on the porch?"

"Yeah. I got it for my birthday. From Mom and Dad."

"It's pretty cool. Maybe one of these days you can show me some skateboard moves. I've always wanted to try."

Something about the way Mom looks at James when he says that makes me look at James in a different way. I'd always figured James was gay. I mean, aren't all male hairdressers gay? Especially the ones who dress fancy? I lean in closer to the table. Mom and James's knees are touching. I can feel my heart starting to race inside my chest.

My mom's been getting it on with her hairdresser. I suddenly remember what Terry said the other day—that he couldn't understand why my mom was hanging out so much at the beauty salon. So Terry must have figured it out before I did.

Now I'm starting to think something else too. James didn't *happen* to drop by the Acropolis. I'll bet the two of them had this planned.

Even though I haven't finished my souvlaki, I get up from the table. "I gotta go," I tell Mom. I make a point of not looking at James.

"Is something wrong?" Mom asks.

That's when I lose it. "He's Honey, isn't he?"

James is standing up now too. "It isn't what you think. Your mom and I really care for each—"

"Stop it!" Mom says to James. "This is no way to explain things to Franklin."

"I gotta go." I think I'm going to be sick.

Bob is still out on the blue and white porch. He's leaning against the railings, counting the stars in the summer sky.

Chapter Nine

On my way home, I notice a bunch of Dad's campaign posters. There he is, beaming at me from telephone and electrical poles along Westminster Avenue. *Ted Westcott Is Your Man*. Maybe, I think, but he isn't his wife's man, not anymore.

I pat my pocket where the matches are. This time, a trash-can fire is not going to satisfy me. I need more flames, more smoke. I need to start a real fire. The thought of all those flames and all that smoke helps take my mind off Mom and you-know-who.

I haven't figured out where to start a bigger fire. I don't want anyone to get hurt. That's not how I operate.

I remember Dad mentioning the abandoned clubhouse on the old golf course. With a little gasoline, that heap of wood would go up in flames. My spine tingles when I picture it.

This fire is going to take more preparation than usual. I'll need to get gasoline. Dad's got an old tin canister in the garage. I could take it to the gas station, tell them we ran out of gas for the truck.

But what if I run into Mr. Cummings? He owns the gas station and is often there till nine or ten at night. If I tell him we've run out of gas, he might say something to Mom or Dad. No, I'd better wait till later.

Dad is on the phone when I get home. He's eating pizza straight from the box. When he sees me, he gives me a thumbs-up. "Big break!" he says, mouthing the words.

"That's terrific news!" I hear Dad say. "The timing couldn't be better—what with the election posters going up. All right then, thanks for everything. We'll all sleep better tonight."

Dad doesn't bother putting the portable phone back on the cradle, the way Mom is always telling us to. He also hasn't kept the newspapers in a neat pile or closed the curtains the way Mom does every night.

He plops down in his easy chair and sighs. "Looks like we caught the guy. I might owe my re-election to Bob."

"Bob?" I ask.

Maybe Bob helped Dad hang posters.

"Yeah. Looks like he's our pyro. The police picked him up for questioning.

They think they've got a positive ID on him from a picture taken the night of the trash-can fire. Turns out all Bob wears is a beat-up black sweatshirt. Plus, witnesses put him at the grass fire on Sunday."

"I don't think Bob—" I stop myself.

"What's that?" Dad asks as he heads into the kitchen.

"Nah, it's nothing," I say. "That's great that you caught the guy."

Dad comes back with a cold beer for himself and a Coke for me. "The timing couldn't be better," he says, sinking back into his chair. He lifts the beer into the air. "Here's to Bob!"

"To Bob!" I add, toasting the poor sucker with my Coke. I wish I could tell Dad about my night. About what a lousy time I had with Mom and how it got lousier after James showed up.

Dad burps. He'd never do that around Mom. Or if he did, he'd apologize.

Dad looks at me. "How'd your mom seem?"

"Fine." It's a dumb answer, but I can't think of a better one.

"Glad to hear it. Hey, did you see any of the election posters on your way home tonight? Waddaya think of that new photograph?"

Dad falls asleep in his easy chair. He has slept in the chair every night since Mom left. I throw out the pizza and put Dad's empty beer bottle and my Coke can in the closet, where Mom stores bottles to return. Who's going to take them back to the store now? We could leave them at the curb and let Bob collect them. But Bob might not be collecting empties for a while, not if he goes to jail.

I try not to make any noise when I go into the garage. The canister is on a shelf at the back near a pile of campaign posters left over from Dad's last election. I shine my flashlight on the old photograph of Dad. He's smiling here too, but the smile looks happier, more relaxed. I wonder when things changed for him—and Mom.

I decide not to go to Mr. Cummings's gas station in case he's working late. Besides, it's a good night for skateboarding, and it will only take me ten more minutes to get to the Petro-Canada on St. Jacques Street. It's close to the highway, so it's popular with truckers. No one there will remember a kid whose dad's truck ran out of gas.

Chapter Ten

The lot at Petro-Can is so full of cars and trucks that I have to wait. One trucker yawns while he fills up. Another stretches his arms. He's probably been driving all day.

When I get a pump, I'm careful not to dribble any gasoline. The sharp smell makes the little hairs inside my nose stand up. Eight dollars' worth. This stuff isn't cheap.

I bring the canister with me into the glass booth where the cashier is. I don't think much of it when I see a head of reddish-brown hair behind the counter. I can't see the cashier's face because she's doing a crossword. It's the hot pink ukulele case on the shelf behind the cash register that clues me in.

"What are you doing here?" I blurt out.

I didn't notice before how green Tracy's eyes are. "What do you mean? I work here. What are *you* doing here?"

"I, uh, came to get some, er, gasoline. My dad ran out of gas. Mom always told him to fill up when the truck's down to a quarter of a tank, but, well, with Mom gone…" I'm babbling. Why do I do that around Tracy?

She gives me a sharp look.

"I was at pump"—I turn around to look out the window and check the number on the pump—"three."

"That'll be eight dollars."

I hand Tracy a ten-dollar bill. "Thanks," I say when she gives me my change.

"Have a nice evening. Come back and see us again." As soon as she says that, Tracy covers her mouth. "Oops, I didn't mean to say that. That's what I'm supposed to say to customers, but you're, well, my friend, kind of."

I like it when Tracy says I'm her friend, even if only *kind of*. I try to think what I can say next. It's probably better not to mention the talent show. "There's been a break in the investigation. They think they caught the pyro."

"Cool!" says Tracy. "I guess you found out from your dad, right? I heard he's the mayor. So who's the pyro? Can you say?"

"They think it's Bob."

"Bob?" Tracy raises her eyebrows. "You're kidding. Bob's the most harmless guy in town. Why would Bob be a pyro?"

"I dunno. Maybe he sets fires to keep warm at night." I laugh at my own joke—even if Tracy doesn't.

"What kind of evidence do they have against him?"

"He was spotted at a bunch of the fires. And some lady took a photo of him the night of the trash-can fire."

"Well, maybe Bob did do it. I feel bad for the guy. I mean he's got nothing. No family, no home. Nothing."

"Look at it this way," I tell Tracy. "They're going to keep him for questioning. So Bob will finally have a roof over his head."

Tracy shakes her head and reaches for her crossword. "Don't you have a heart, Franklin?" she mutters.

I figure that is not the sort of question that requires an answer. Instead, I try to change the subject, move on to something lighter. "I see you brought your ukulele to work."

"You're very observant." Tracy doesn't say this in a nice way. Maybe she's still ticked off about what I said about Bob.

Two truckers are on their way into the booth. They stop, and one of them lights a cigarette. "What time do you finish?" I ask Tracy. "D'you want me to stick around and make sure you get home safe?"

Tracy gives me a sideways look. Maybe now she doesn't think I'm heartless. "Nah, you don't have to. Besides, isn't your dad waiting for that gasoline?"

Shoot! I completely forgot that story I told her. "Uh, yeah, you're right. I gotta get back. But I—I could come around later to get you."

Tracy checks the time on her cell phone. "I'm working till eleven. Are you sure that's not too late?"

"I can make it work. I'll, uh, come back after we get the truck started."

It's nearly ten thirty. That gives me just enough time to stash the canister in the garage. I'll need to hurry if I want to meet up with Tracy. And I want to meet up with Tracy.

"Okay, I'll see you in a bit," Tracy says.

The two truckers are at the door now.

"Hey, Franklin," Tracy says. "What'd you do to your hair? It looks like you burned it."

Chapter Eleven

I put the canister away in the garage. I get so busy thinking about Tracy, I lose track of my fire-starting plan. But I know I'll get the urge again. I always do. And next time, I'll be ready.

From outside, I can see the gray light from our TV. I let myself in and take a pee in the downstairs bathroom. I check out my reflection in the mirror. My hair does look like I burned it. One part of my bangs looks wispy, like it was cut with sewing shears. I use the nail scissors by the sink to even up my hair. It's lucky no one else noticed. Not even Mom or Dad—or James.

I wonder if Tracy would ever kiss a guy like me. I might not be tall, but I'm no monster. Then I remember how Tracy asked if I had a heart. That is probably not the best sign. Girls want to kiss guys who have hearts. Guys like James.

When I get back to the Petro-Can, Tracy is waiting at the door, her ukulele case tucked under her arm. She smells like gasoline, but I don't mention it. I figure it's not the kind of thing a guy should tell a girl he's interested in.

"Everything go okay with your dad's truck?" Tracy asks.

"It's all good."

I carry my skateboard so I can walk next to Tracy. Tomorrow is recycling day.

Some of the green boxes take up half the sidewalk, overflowing with newspapers and bottles. It's the kind of thing that would usually bug me. Tonight it doesn't, because it means I get to walk closer to Tracy, so close that sometimes our elbows touch. Tracy could pull back when that happens, but she doesn't.

"It's nice that you came all the way back to walk with me," Tracy says.

"No problem. A girl shouldn't be walking alone on St. Jacques Street this time of night."

"Maybe you do have a heart."

I can feel myself smiling in the darkness. "Maybe I do."

"What you said about Bob wasn't nice."

I guess Tracy isn't the type to let things slide. "I was just joking around."

"It still wasn't nice."

I don't know if I'm supposed to apologize, so I don't. We walk for a bit without saying anything. It's not the bad kind of quiet that makes the air heavy and tense, the kind I got used to in our house. This is the kind of quiet that lets you appreciate the sound of the crickets and the shuffle of your footsteps on the sidewalk.

"How're things going at your house?" Tracy asks.

My shoulders tense. "Okay, I guess."

Tracy doesn't let this topic slide either. "It must be hard."

"It is kinda hard."

"Do you miss her?"

"Uh-huh." I feel this awful lump in my throat. I swallow hard to make it go away. "I'd rather not talk about it. If you don't mind."

"Sure thing. I'm sorry. I didn't mean to pry."

"Don't worry about it."

Tracy lives just past the "hump," a steep section of Westminster Avenue near the northern edge of town. On our way, we pass a row of red brick low-rise apartments. Most of the balconies have flower boxes. One even has potted tomato plants.

At first, when I hear Mom's laugh, I'm not sure where it's coming from. Maybe I'm imagining it. I hear the laugh again and realize it's coming from the parking lot beside the apartments.

I think about crossing to the other side of the street. But it's too late. Mom, who is carrying a box in her arms, has spotted me.

What's surprising is the weird look on her face. She looks like she wishes she'd crossed the street too. "Fr— Franklin," she says. "I didn't expect to see you here. Oh, I see you're with a friend." Mom rests the cardboard box against her belly so she can shake Tracy's hand.

"Nice to meet you, Mrs. Westcott," Tracy says.

Now someone else appears out of the shadows. It's James. He's carrying another box. Mom's car keys are hanging from his lips. I recognize the cupcake keychain.

"Hey, Franklin!" James says. "Nice to see you hanging out with a lady. Cute one too!"

I want to throttle James. Right now.

But Tracy's not embarrassed. "I'm Tracy," she says, which reminds me that I should have introduced her. "I work at the Petro-Can. Franklin offered to walk me home."

Now James does something worse. He winks! Then he says, "Our Franklin's quite the charmer."

"I'm not *your* Franklin." Everyone else gets really quiet after I say that. Not the good quiet.

"Of course you're not," James says.

"What's in the boxes?" Tracy asks.

I wish she hadn't asked. I don't want to know the answer. "We should get going," I say, tugging on the sleeve of Tracy's jacket.

"Moira's stuff. She's moving in with me," James says.

I get that sick feeling in my stomach again. She's moving in with him? Couldn't she have waited awhile? This means Mom definitely won't be moving back home.

"So you live in this building?" Tracy asks James.

"That's my apartment." James gestures to a corner balcony on the first floor. "The one with the tomato plants."

"James has a green thumb," Mom says.

I want to say that James is a smarmy wife-stealing, mom-stealing jerk. I've never been so angry at anyone in all my life. Mom is a complete idiot to fall for him and his tomatoes.

But I've never been the sort of person who says what I really think.

Mom wants to know if I'd come for dinner at the apartment next week.

"I'll see," I say.

I want to leave, but James won't let me. "We'd really like to have you over, Franklin," he says. I wish he wouldn't use the word *we* like that. When I try backing away, James just steps closer. "You're going to love my stuffed tomato recipe," he says. "I use my own tomatoes. I only make them for my favorite people."

I don't want to be one of James's favorite people. Not next week. Not ever.

"I'm really looking forward to bonding with you, Franklin," James adds.

In the end, Tracy saves me. She points to the boxes Mom and James are carrying and then to the tomato plants. "I think all of this is a lot for Franklin right now."

Chapter Twelve

Tracy is right. Finding out that Mom is moving in with her hairdresser is a lot for me to handle. Maybe that's why I can't concentrate. Tracy is telling me about how she got into playing ukulele. I'm nodding and saying "Uh-huh," but nothing registers.

When we get to Tracy's house, she punches my shoulder and disappears inside before I can try to kiss her good night. Maybe it's just as well. This doesn't feel like the right kind of night for kissing.

It feels like the right kind of night for starting a fire.

Since we ran into Mom and James, I haven't been able to think of anything else. I fly home on my skateboard picturing that canister in the garage. I can feel its weight and smell the gasoline. It's not that I want to start a fire. I need to.

I'm skating so fast I nearly crash into the garage door.

When I hoist open the door, my eyes land on the canister. I'm breathing quickly now, and my heart is pounding. *Ba-dum. Ba-dum.*

It isn't easy to skateboard with a canister of gasoline. It requires good balance. Luckily, I can do it. I can't go as quickly as I want to, but nothing can stop me. The impulse is bigger than me.

My breathing starts to settle down, but my heart is still pounding. I'm already halfway to the old golf course. When I hit a crack in the road, a little gasoline spills on the pavement.

It's dark at the golf course. It's a good thing I grabbed a flashlight from the garage. I wade through the tall grass. There's no grass where I started my last fire. The old shed isn't far. Long ago, when the golf club had lots of members, they came to the shed for drinks and snacks.

The beam of my flashlight lands on the shed, or what's left of it. There's a stone foundation and remnants of the structure. It's basically a lean-to of old gray boards. They will be perfect kindling.

For a second, I think I hear someone humming. But when I strain my ears to hear better, I decide it's a bird. Maybe birds make their nests in the tall grass.

I drop my skateboard and make my way to the shed. It's hard to imagine that fancy people used to hang out here. I wonder where they all are now. Dead, probably.

I hold the canister like I'm watering plants. This reminds me of James and his stupid tomatoes. A drop of gasoline lands on one of my sneakers, and I rub the toe in the dirt to get rid of the oily spot.

It doesn't take long to empty the canister. I'm on autopilot when I reach for my matches. I kick at the old wooden boards to create space between them. Like Dad used to tell me, a good fire needs oxygen.

I can already imagine the *whoosh* this fire will make when it ignites. I'm about to strike the match when I notice something on the ground I didn't see before. It's a dented steel thermos and a blue tin plate. The plate has bits of dried food on it. Someone must have used it not long ago.

A terrible thought crosses my mind. Could this abandoned lean-to be somebody's house?

Bob. This could be where Bob comes to sleep! That thermos and plate might belong to him. And if it isn't Bob's place, it must belong to somebody like him.

I remember my conversation with Tracy. *So Bob'll finally have a roof over his head.* But this abandoned clubhouse *is* the roof over Bob's head. *Don't you have a heart, Franklin?* Do I?

When I hear the fire engine's siren, I think I'm dreaming. Why is the fire brigade coming here? I haven't even started the fire. It's as if they knew what I was planning.

I look toward where the sound is coming from. I expect to see the fire engine's red, white and yellow lights burning in the night, but I don't see them.

The fire engine is headed some-where else.

Someone has set another fire in Montreal West.

Chapter Thirteen

I grab my skateboard and jump on as soon as I reach the road. At first, I follow the siren's wail. The air is warm, but my arms get cold when I see the fire engine's lights and realize how close this fire is to the town center. It's only a block or two from the town hall, where Dad works.

The fire is on Percival Avenue, near the train tracks. As I round the corner,

I remember the old clapboard house on Percival. It's had a For Sale sign outside for as long as I can remember, and some of the downstairs windows are smashed.

It's after midnight, but there are a dozen or so people outside. Most are wearing pajamas or bathrobes. They're not paying much attention to the clapboard house, not even when its roof collapses. They're focused on the small red-brick house next door. Flames are licking at one side of it.

"I sure hope the Campbells get out okay," I hear a woman say.

There's only one oxygen tank left hanging on the side of the fire engine. The firefighters must have taken the others.

Two firefighters emerge from the house, their faces covered with soot. One firefighter, Jeff's friend Terry, is leading Mr. Campbell by the arm. The other firefighter is carrying Mrs. Campbell.

The crowd cheers. They take the Campbells over to the ambulance waiting near the front of the house. The paramedics rush out and load the Campbells onto stretchers.

"I think Mrs. Campbell's passed out," someone whispers.

Mr. Campbell is sobbing—and pointing at the house. "What is it?" I hear a paramedic ask him.

"It's Gabrielle. My granddaughter. She's still inside!"

For a moment, it's as if the crowd is one person gasping for air.

The other firefighters are dousing both houses with water. But the flames that were licking at the side of the Campbells' house are making their way up to the second floor, reaching up and curling like claws around the red brick.

"I'm going in to get Gabrielle!" a voice calls through the smoke.

Mr. Campbell is sobbing and shaking his head. He's saying he won't leave until Gabrielle is safe.

"Where is Gabrielle? What room is she in?" someone shouts.

Mr. Campbell has trouble finding his words.

"I don't know what he's saying!" one of the paramedics calls out.

Though he's strapped to the stretcher, Mr. Campbell manages to wave his hands. "We need to give him a sedative," I hear the paramedic say. His voice sounds panicky. Paramedics aren't supposed to panic, are they?

"Not yet." The other paramedic sounds calmer. "Not until we know where Gabrielle is."

The second paramedic leans over the stretcher. He look right into Mr. Campbell's eyes and speaks to him in a loud, clear voice. "Where's Gabrielle?"

Mr. Campbell coughs. His whole face has turned gray. "She's in the den," he sputters. "Near the kitchen."

The second paramedic is yelling now, repeating Mr. Campbell's words. And his words are getting repeated throughout the crowd. "Tell Terry!" I hear someone shout. "Gabrielle's in the den. Near the kitchen!"

One paramedic gets into the driver's seat. The other hops inside and slams the ambulance doors shut. The ambulance disappears into the night. More sirens. Another ambulance must be coming for Gabrielle. If the firefighters can get her out in time.

Those of us waiting on the curb huddle close. A woman drops to her knees and prays out loud for Gabrielle. "Please, Lord..."

"Do you suppose it was an electrical fire?" someone whispers.

"No way," I say. "Can't you smell the gasoline?"

"Who would do something like this?" someone else asks.

After that, no one speaks—or even whispers. We're all watching the Campbells' house. Is that Terry's shadow moving around inside?

A car pulls up, screeching its brakes, and then there is this awful desperate crying. Someone says it's the Campbells' daughter, Gabrielle's mom. She wants to go inside the burning house, but people at the front of the crowd hold her back.

This is more emotion than I can take. I want to get away, but I also want to know what's going to happen. I've never been religious, but I'm praying in my head. *Please, Lord, let Gabrielle be okay.*

There's more crying and shouting as Terry stumbles out of the house, Gabrielle in his arms.

"I've got her!" From behind the oxygen mask, Terry's voice comes out like a croak.

Gabrielle lets out a wail, and the whole crowd cheers.

Gabrielle's mom cradles her baby. There's another paramedic on the scene. "We need to check the baby's vital signs," this paramedic says, taking Gabrielle from her mom. People are hugging Terry and thanking him for being so brave.

"If the Montreal Fire Department doesn't give him a job now, they never will," someone says.

The damage to the Campbells' house is serious, but no one was hurt, and the flames are finally dying down.

When Dad shows up, I slip to the back of the crowd. One good thing about being short is that it's easy to get lost in a crowd. I don't want Dad to spot me here in the middle of the night. I hear the chief of the volunteer squad filling Dad in on what's happened.

"Let me see Terry," Dad says.

I move in a little closer so I can see what happens next. Dad hugs Terry hard. "Thanks for what you've done for our community."

Everyone claps.

Everyone, that is, except me.

Chapter Fourteen

When I can't sleep, I google *fire*. I read about the history of fire, fire-starting tricks, fire in mythology. Tonight I'm looking at firefighting sites, and my eyes land on a word I've never seen before. *Backfire*.

It's a technique used to escape from a wildfire. Sometimes it's called back-burn or escape fire. The technique was used in 1949 at the Mann Gulch fire in Montana's Helena National Forest. Thirteen people died at Mann Gulch, including twelve guys who were parachuted onto the scene.

This guy named Wagner Dodge figured the only way to protect himself and his crew from the fire was by lighting another fire. So he burned an area of grass and ordered his crew to lie down on the scorched earth. Some of them thought Dodge had lost his mind. But when the bigger fire reached them, Dodge and his men were safe.

I'm thinking about backfires and Montana when I hear Dad come home. He's on the phone, I'm guessing with the police chief. "I'm glad you had him under surveillance. But if Bob didn't set that fire tonight, who did?"

In the morning, the smell of coffee wakes me. There are voices in the kitchen.

Could Mom be back? No, the voice that isn't Dad's belongs to a man.

Who would drop by so early in the morning? Maybe the police chief.

It's 8:30, and I've got my first weeding job at nine. I throw on some clothes, make a quick bathroom stop and head to the kitchen.

Someone's in my chair. I step back when I see who it is. What is Terry doing here?

Dad and Terry must be having an intense conversation, because neither of them notices I'm standing three feet away. Dad's rubbing his temples.

"Look, Mayor Westcott," Terry says, "it wasn't easy for me to come here this morning, but I knew I had to. He's your kid."

"What's going on?" I ask.

Terry gets up from my chair when he sees me. "I'd better get going," he says, without looking at me. He turns back to my dad. "So you're okay to write that letter of recommendation for me, Mr. Mayor? I'm sure it'd help a lot. I'd do anything to get a job with the Montreal Fire Department."

"I'd be glad to write that letter, Terry." Only Dad doesn't sound too glad. He doesn't bother getting up to let Terry out. He just takes a long sip of coffee. His eyes look tired. "It looks like we have ourselves a problem, Franklin. A big problem."

My first thought is that Dad is finally going to talk to me about Mom's new living arrangements.

But that isn't it at all.

"Terry says he saw you at the fire last night and he reminded me that you were also at the grass fire at the old golf course. In fact"—Dad is clutching his coffee mug so tight, his knuckles are white— "he says you never miss a fire. What do you have to say for yourself, Franklin?"

It's as if my heart is beating in my throat. "I didn't start that fire last night, Dad."

Dad puts down his mug. "How do I know you're not lying, Franklin?"

"You don't."

I take a piece of bread out of the bag and pop it in the toaster. I hope Dad can't see I'm shaking.

Then, without even saying where he's going, Dad walks out of the kitchen and leaves the house. Could he be moving out too?

I hear the garage door open and the sounds of Dad poking around inside.

"Franklin!" Dad shouts so loud, I'm sure the whole street can hear him. "Where the hell is that canister I use for gasoline?"

Shoot! I must've left the canister at the golf course. What do I tell Dad? I don't want to lie, but I can't tell the truth either. So I do the only thing I can think of—I slip out the front door and take off on my skateboard.

I don't plan to go to Tracy's. I just end up there. Tracy's mom is outside, watering the lawn. She has the same hair color as Tracy.

"Are you a friend of Tracy's?" she asks when I skateboard up.

I shake her hand because I know adults like it when you do that. "Yeah, we're friends. From Sunday school. I'm Franklin."

"Lovely to meet you. Tracy told us all about you. She said you walked her home last night. Thanks for doing that, Franklin. You sound like a real gentleman."

Tracy must hear us, because she pops her head out of an upstairs window and says, "Don't you have gardens to weed?"

"Yeah. But I need to talk to you. If you don't mind."

"How 'bout if I meet you at your first garden—in about fifteen minutes?"

I agree and give Tracy directions.

I'm weeding when she shows up. This late in the summer, there aren't too many dandelions left. I'm mostly tearing out hunks of crabgrass. Tracy wants to help.

"So what'd you want to talk to me about?" she asks as she pulls up a handful of crabgrass.

I don't look at her when I answer. "My dad thinks I started that fire last night. He thinks I started all the fires."

Tracy puts her hand on my shoulder. "Did you?"

"I sometimes start fires," I tell her. "But I'm not the pyro." It's the closest I've come to telling anyone the truth. It feels better than I expected. "I'd never light a fire that might hurt someone."

"There's always a chance someone might get hurt." Tracy's voice is stern.

I put down my trowel and look at Tracy. She's right. Someone might get hurt. I know how it works for me. Every fire has to be bigger than the last one. What if it's the same for the pyro? "I need to catch the pyro," I tell her.

"How're you going to do that?"

"I need to think like a pyro."

Tracy cracks a smile. "That shouldn't be hard for you."

Chapter Fifteen

Dad comes by at lunch. He brings me apple juice and a tuna sandwich. I don't tell him there's too much mayo in the tuna.

"I looked on your laptop, Franklin."

He doesn't seem to feel too guilty about it. "You spend an awful lot of time reading about fires. I spoke to your mom. We want you to see someone so you can talk about your feelings."

"What if I don't want to?"

"You have to, Franklin. Like it or not."

I spend the afternoon weeding and thinking. If Bob didn't light last night's fire, and I didn't light it, who did? And why would someone light a fire that could hurt people?

That's when the lightbulb goes off.

Terry.

Didn't he say he'd do anything to work for the Montreal Fire Department?

When I get home, I call Tracy and ask her to meet me at 9:00 PM.

Terry lives in a brick house on Wolseley Avenue. A bumper sticker on a garage window reads *Firefighters can take the heat.*

The garage is locked. "Too bad!" I whisper. "I wanted to see what Terry's got in there."

"Maybe I can help," Tracy says, grinning as she pulls out a bobby pin from behind one ear.

"You know how to pick locks?"

"Picking locks is chapter four in the *Ukulele for Beginners* handbook," Tracy says.

"You're kidding, right?"

"Right," says Tracy. "We've got an old garage too. Mom lost the key, so we use a bobby pin instead. Here, let me show you."

Tracy is about to insert her bobby pin in the lock when we hear a vehicle pull up. I grab Tracy, and we duck behind some bushes.

We try to not even breathe as Terry pulls in. He gets out of his truck to unlock the garage door. Then he turns on a light. From our hiding spot, we can see the inside of the garage. There's shelving along the walls. The shelving on the far wall holds three large cans of gasoline, lined up like soldiers.

Terry looks around to make sure no one's watching. Then he grabs two cans of gasoline and stashes them in the back of the truck. After that, he goes into his house.

I gesture for Tracy to follow me. I can tell she understands what we're going to do next.

I keep an eye on Terry's front door as I help Tracy into the back of the truck. Then I hop up too. There are plenty of blankets to hide under. We get as far away as possible from the cans of gas.

"I don't get it," Tracy whispers. "Why would a firefighter start fires?"

"If he's a big enough hero, he'll have a better chance of getting hired by the city."

"That's sick."

There's no telling how long Terry will be inside. I'm cramping up, and the blanket feels scratchy. There is one benefit to this. I'm so close to Tracy, I can hear her breathe.

Neither of us says anything for a bit, then Tracy breaks the silence. "Why do *you* start fires, Franklin?"

"It helps when I'm"—I stop to find the right word—"anxious."

"You're going to have to stop."

"I know."

We hear Terry slam his front door shut. He whistles as he gets into the truck and starts the engine.

I try to make out where we're going from the way the truck swerves.

Are we on Westminster Avenue?

When I peek out from under the blanket, I see we're right in front of James's place. Correction. James and Mom's place.

Why would Terry start a fire here?

Oh no! I think as the answer comes to me. Terry must have figured out how

I feel about James and Mom. He's going to start a fire at their apartment and pin it on me. No wonder he's whistling.

Tracy and I huddle close. I think we're both wondering what Terry will do if he finds us. But he doesn't. He grabs a can of gasoline.

I don't have to peek out from under the blanket to know what he's doing now. He's dousing the ground with gasoline.

"Let's go!" I tell Tracy. We scramble to the ground, trying not to make too much noise. We stay behind the truck so that if Terry looks around, he won't see us.

If we peer out from behind the truck, we can see him. Tracy takes out her cell phone to call 9-1-1. Her hands are shaking.

Terry is on James's balcony. I know because of the tomato plants. Things are moving so quickly now that it's hard for me to keep track. Tracy is talking to the 9-1-1 operator. Terry starts the fire.

It catches quickly, thanks to the gasoline. At first, it's a glowing ball, and then the ball gets bigger and more orange. Fiery puddles form on the balcony floor.

Mom's not in the apartment. At least, I don't see her car in the parking lot. Maybe she's gone to buy groceries.

Terry will need to flee the scene. I watch as he stops to look at the fire. I know what he's thinking, because I've thought it too. *That's my fire. I made it.*

It's only a step down to the lawn that borders the apartment. Terry will be back behind the wheel in a minute or so. I know what will happen after that too. In about fifteen minutes, he'll turn up in his volunteer firefighter's uniform, ready to play the hero.

Terry turns to step down to the lawn, and his eyes land on me. First, he looks surprised. Then he starts to laugh. "Hey, squirt!" he calls to me. "You're making this too easy! Imagine that!

Here you are, setting fire to your mom's boyfriend's place!"

Terry is laughing so hard, he has to wipe his eyes. That's when he loses his balance. He bangs his head on the edge of the balcony. A tomato plant topples at the same time Terry does.

"Oh my god," Tracy says, "his foot!"

Terry's foot is caught in the railing. The weird thing is, he's not trying to get it loose.

"I think he knocked himself out," Tracy says. "The fire truck better get here soon. We need an ambulance too."

Tracy is back on her phone when I start running toward the balcony. "Franklin!" she calls out after me. "Don't!"

Terry tried to frame me. Even so, I can't stand there and watch the fire get to him. The flames are awfully close to him now. "Terry!" I scream. I think I can reach his foot from here. "Wake up!"

I shout. But he's still out cold. Maybe he's inhaled too much smoke.

The smoke is making me cough now too. First, I need to get his foot out from between the railings. It's not easy, but I manage.

Where's the fire truck? I'm waiting for the sound of the siren, but I don't hear it.

There's someone else nearby. It's too smoky for me to see who it is. But I need to get up on the balcony to reach Terry. I cover my mouth and hoist myself up with my other hand. I can hear the other person getting up on the balcony too. "We need to get him out of here," I manage to say.

I grab Terry's feet. "You take his head," I say.

"I'll try."

"Tracy?"

For a girl with stage fright, Tracy is amazing. I hear her panting and coughing. Or is that me panting and coughing?

Or is it Terry? I'm afraid I'm going to pass out too.

Yet somehow, Tracy and I manage to drag Terry out of danger just as the fire engine comes flying down the street.

The last thing I hear before I do pass out is my father's voice. "What the heck is going on here?"

Chapter Sixteen

Who knew I'd have a talent for stage lighting?

Jeff says there's lots of work on movie sets for lighting technicians. The really good techies sometimes even get to be lighting directors in Hollywood.

Right now, I've got the spotlight on Tracy's hands. She's strumming the ukulele. Her voice sounds good. Confident.

I'm pretty sure Tracy has her stage-fright thing beat.

I'm working on my fire-starting thing.

Dr. Ford, the psychologist Dad and Mom forced me to see, isn't a bad guy. For one thing, he's really interested in fires and how they work. I asked him if he ever set fires when he was a kid. He didn't say yes, but he didn't say no either, which makes me think maybe he did. Only I guess it wouldn't be very professional if he told me so.

Jeff is home for Christmas. He's sitting in the third row, next to Mom and James. Dad is in the front row, of course. Where else would the mayor sit? He says I helped him win the election.

Terry is in jail. Dr. Ford and I talk about him sometimes. I know that if I don't get the fire starting under control, I could end up there too.

Even after everything Terry did or tried to do to me, I still hope he gets help while he's in prison. Dr. Ford thinks it's a good sign that I feel that way. He says it shows that I'm developing empathy, which is another way of saying that I've got a heart.

No matter how old I get to be, I know I'll always be amazed by fire. Dr. Ford says that's okay too.

"Fire is elemental," he said in our session last week. "Perhaps that's why it captures the human imagination."

That reminded me of something Dad used to say when I was a little kid, watching him start a fire in our fireplace—"Fire creates, but it destroys too."

This summer, a lot of stuff got destroyed, but other stuff—good stuff, hopeful stuff—got created.

Acknowledgments

A big thank you to all the young people I've met during school visits who have shared their stories about playing with fire.

Special thanks to Dr. Kenneth R. Fineman, a California psychologist who treats young firestarters, and who made time to answer my questions.

Many thanks also to my friends at the Kahnawake Fire Brigade. Firefighter John Rice gave me a great tour of the station and introduced me to the world of firefighting. Assistant Fire Chief Bryan Deer and firefighter Cheryl Montour patiently answered further questions.

Thanks to the wonderful team at Orca Book Publishers, especially Melanie Jeffs for her fine editor's eye and ear.

Thanks, too, to my friend Viva Singer, for letting me talk out another story. So did my husband Michael Shenker and my daughter Alicia Melamed. I love you both too much.

Monique Polak has written numerous novels for youth. Many of them are, like *Pyro*, set in the Montreal area, where she lives and teaches English and Humanities at Marianopolis College. Monique also works as a freelance journalist.

orca *currents*

For more information on all the books
in the Orca Currents series, please visit
www.orcabook.com